# SOL A SOL

Bilingual Poems Written and Selected by Lori Marie Carlson

Illustrated by Emily Lisker

Henry Holt and Company   New York

Henry Holt and Company, LLC, *Publishers since 1866*, 115 West 18th Street, New York, New York 10011
Henry Holt is a registered trademark of Henry Holt and Company, LLC
Text copyright © 1998 by Lori Marie Carlson. Illustrations copyright © 1998 by Emily Lisker. All rights reserved.
Distributed in Canada by H. B. Fenn and Company Ltd.
Library of Congress Cataloging-in-Publication Data
Sol a sol: bilingual poems / written and selected by Lori Marie Carlson; illustrated by Emily Lisker.
English and Spanish. Summary: A collection of poems by various Hispanic-American writers that celebrate a full day of family activities.
1. Family—Juvenile poetry.  2. Children's poetry, American—Translations into Spanish.  3. Children's poetry, Hispanic
American (Spanish)—Translations into English. [1. Family life—Poetry.  2. American poetry—Hispanic American
authors—Collections.  3. Spanish language materials—Bilingual.]  I. Carlson, Lori M.  II. Lisker, Emily, ill.
PS595.F34S65   1998   811'.540809282—dc21   97-18574
ISBN 0-8050-4373-X / First Edition—1998 / Typography by Martha Rago
The artist used acrylic paint on canvas to create the illustrations for this book.
Printed in Hong Kong
3  5  7  9  10  8  6  4

Permission for use of the following is gratefully acknowledged: Marjorie Agosín for her poem excerpt from "Papas," retitled "Peeling Potatoes with Papi."
Copyright © 1998 by Marjorie Agosin. Reprinted by her permission. Gustavo Gatti for his poem "Tu Aroma," retitled "Mami." Copyright © 1998 by
Gustavo Gatti. Reprinted by his permission. Alexis González for his poem "Lizards." Copyright © 1998 by Alexis González. Reprinted by permission of
Dr. Joan Lunney, principal of P.S. 119. Henry Quintero for his poem excerpt from "Making Tortillas." Copyright © 1993 by the Antioch Review, Inc.
First appeared in the *Antioch Review* 51, no. 3 (summer 1993). Reprinted by permission of the editors. Yolanda, *Just Born Poems,* Vol. VIII, 1993; *An
Anthology of Poetry,* written by the Children of St. Mary's Hospital for Children, Bayside, New York, and published by Poets in Public Service, Inc. Every
effort has been made to contact copyright holders. The publisher would be happy to hear from any copyright holders not acknowledged or acknowledged
incorrectly.

To my mom and dad, Marie and Robert,
whose bedtime stories, hugs, and tickles
I remember in the glow of sunsets now in New York City,
so many suns later
— L . M . C .

To Bill Calhoun
— E . L .

☆ ✩ ☆

*Sol a Sol,* abbreviated from "de sol a sol," means sunup to
sundown, a day. I wanted my bilingual poetry collection to be
as linked and as varied as morning, noon, and night. First I
picked poems I liked, then I added my own as a kind of ribbon
to wrap our voices together. My friend Lyda Aponte de Zacklin
translated most of the poetry into Spanish and made sure each
poem can be read as well in Spanish as it can in English.
— L . M . C .

## Mama

You smell like milk that's spilled.

You smell like honey.

You smell like bread and mint

and the freshness of the morning.


## Mami

Hueles a leche derramada.

Hueles a miel de abeja.

Hueles a pan, a menta

y a frágil madrugada.

—Gustavo Gatti
*translated from the Spanish*
*by L. M. C.*

## Making Tortillas

When my mother makes tortillas
for my father and for me,
the steel chimes, the rock pings and rattles
with each pass over the dough.
My mother tells me that her rolling pin is
singing *I love you, I love you.*

## Haciendo tortillas

Cuando mi mamá hace tortillas
para papá y para mí
el acero repica, la piedra zumba y matraquea
con cada amasadura de la masa.
Mi mamá me dice que su rodillo
está cantando *te quiero, te quiero.*

—Henry Quintero
*translated from the English*
*by L. A. Z.*

## Garden Footprints

I leave footprints
on the gravel path to
mama's garden full of *calabazas,*
*tomates, girasoles.*
Footprints
leading to and from this place,
where mama spends her afternoons
beneath a hat so big it
shades me too
while
I kneel down and
help plant flowers.

## Huellas de jardín

Dejo huellas
en el sendero pedregoso hacia
el jardín de mamá lleno de calabazas,
tomates, girasoles.
Huellas
que llevan hacia y desde este lugar
donde mi mamá pasa sus tardes
debajo de un sombrero tan grande
que me resguarda a mí también
mientras me arrodillo y
ayudo a sembrar flores.

— Lori Marie Carlson
*translated from the English*
*by L. A. Z.*

# My Grandmother

My grandmother
    is a honey-colored woman
    warm as the sand
        on her tropical island
My grandmother
    is a tall straight woman
    swaying like the palms
        on her tropical island
My grandmother
    is a talking woman
    chattering like the green parrots
        on her tropical island
My grandmother
    sweet sugarcane woman
    I love her so.

# Mi abuela

Mi abuela
    es una mujer color de almíbar
    cálida como la arena
        de su isla tropical.
Mi abuela
    es una mujer alta y esbelta
    balanceándose como las palmas
        de su isla tropical.
Mi abuela
    es una mujer habladora
    como los pericos
        de su isla tropical.
Mi abuela
    dulce mujer de cañamiel
    yo la quiero así.

—Pela Chacón
*translated from the English*
*by L. A. Z.*

# El abuelo canta

Mi abuelo señala hacia arriba
y dice: "¡Mira! un cielito lindo."
Y mientras toca su vieja guitarra,
Veo
sus cejas finas volar
su diente de oro chasquear
su manzana de Adam subir y bajar
los vellos de su nariz estornudar
su dedo gordo encogerse

Sólo nosotros bajo un árbol de algodón
a cantar
ay, ay, ay, ay.

# Grandpa Singing

Grandpa points above him
and says: "Now, there's a *cielito lindo.*"
And while he plays his old guitar,
I watch
his wispy eyebrows flying
his gold tooth chomping
his Adam's apple bobbing
his hairy nostrils sneezing
his big toe curling

Just the two of us beneath a cotton tree
singing
*ay, ay, ay, ay.*

— Lori Marie Carlson
*translated from the English*
*by L. A. Z.*

## Lizards

Behind my grandfather's house
    there is a hill
    where I catch baby lizards.
I let them bite my ears
    so I can wear them
    like earrings.

## Lagartos

Detrás de la casa de mi abuelo
    hay una colina
    donde agarro a los bebé lagartos.
Dejo que me muerdan las orejas
    para poder llevarlos
    como aretes.

—Alexis González
*translated from the English*
*by L. A. Z.*

## Chocolate

From sunny morning
till moony night
I eat
chocolate. It doesn't matter
if it's chocolate milk or chocolate doughnuts
chocolate candy bars or chocolate cake
or even chicken à la chocolate.
All that matters is
the dark, sweet taste of
cinnamon, cocoa, almonds, cream
melting
on
my
tongue.

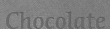

## Chocolate

Desde la mañana asoleada
hasta la noche de luna
Como
chocolate. No importa
si es chocolate de leche o buñuelo de chocolate
bombones de chocolate o torta de chocolate
o incluso pollo a la chocolate.
Lo que importa es
el secreto, dulce sabor a
canela, cocoa, almendras, crema
derritiéndose
en
mi
lengua.

# I Like to Ride My Bike

I'm ready
for a bike ride. I wear
long blue shorts, my red helmet and
a white T-shirt hanging to my knees.
One pedal
spins
and then, I'm off!

Leaves blur into green air
people shout hello, be careful
stay on the sidewalk.

The wind cools my arms
and legs.
I feel free.

## Me gusta montar mi bicicleta

Estoy lista para mi paseo en bicicleta. Llevo
mis largas bermudas azules, mi casco rojo y
una camiseta blanca colgando hasta las rodillas.
Un pedal
gira
y luego, ¡parto!

Las hojas se desvanecen en el verdor del aire
La gente grita ¡Hola! ten cuidado
quédate en la acera.

El viento refresca mis brazos
y piernas.
Me siento libre.

—Lori Marie Carlson
*translated from the English*
*by  L. A. Z.*

## The Wind Bragging

Anthony sounds like the wind
    bragging in the air.
Danille sounds like a clock ticking.
Yelitza sounds like a bird singing outside.

Sophia sounds like a cat purring.
Christine sounds like a piano playing.
Tai sounds like a basketball bouncing.
Bianca sounds like rap music played
    by Shai.

# El viento jactancioso

Anthony suena como el viento
    que se jacta en el aire.
Danille suena como tic-tac de reloj.
Yelitza suena como un pájaro
    cantando afuera.

Sophía suena como un gato runruneando.
Christine suena como un piano tocando.
Tai suena como un baloncesto rebotando.
Bianca suena como música de rap interpretada
    por Shai.

—Yolanda
*translated from the English*
*by L. A. Z.*

## Gato

He's a free flip
of fur
gray, soft somersault
and then a careful landing
on four polished paws
followed by the chachachá. That's
Gato, my best friend.

## Gato

Es un manotazo suelto
de piel
gris, vuelta de carnero suave
y luego un aterrizaje cuidadoso
en cuatro garras pulidas
seguido del chachachá. Este es
Gato, mi mejor amigo.

—Lori Marie Carlson
*translated from the English*
*by* L. A. Z.

## Pelando papas con papi

Papa

Papaita,

patata, batata

pareces una risa con ojos

con rostros desgarbados, oscuros, luminosos

dorada.

## Peeling Potatoes with Papi

Potatoes,

papas,

papaitas, patatas, batatas

you look like laughter with eyes,

with lopsided faces, dark, luminous,

golden.

—Marjorie Agosín
*translated from the Spanish
by Cola Franzen*

## Shuffle, Jump

After dinner
papa rolls the rugs
and pushes them against the wall.
The sofas, chairs, tiny tables too.
In the living room
the lights dim.
Papa plays good music
and mama
slides, slides, slides into
a twirl. They say to me,
"Let's dance."
And we shuffle, jump,
let our hips kiss to the music.

## Moverse, saltar

Después de la cena, papá enrolla las alfombras
y las empuja contra la pared juntas con
los sofás, sillas y mesitas también.
En la sala las luces oscurecen
Papá toca música bailable
y mamá, se desliza, desliza hasta
dar vueltas. Ellos me dicen:
—¡Bailemos!
Y nosotros nos movemos, saltamos,
dejamos a nuestras caderas besarse con la música.

—Lori Marie Carlson
translated from the English
by L. A. Z.

# The Smell of Night

I climb into bed

look out the window

framed by mama's handmade curtains, dark

velvet next to setting sun

of orange, deep red like *manzanas*

and I think I can smell

that setting sun

like an overripe mango or peach

waiting to be eaten.

# El olor de la noche

Me subo a la cama

miro por la ventana

enmarcada por las cortinas hechas a mano por mamá,

terciopelo oscuro junto a la puesta de sol

anaranjado, rojo profundo

como manzanas

y pienso que puede oler

la puesta de sol

como un mango maduro o durazno

esperando a ser comidos.

—Lori Marie Carlson
*translated from the English*
*by L. A. Z.*

## Stars

Through the window
night stars wait.
I count
uno, dos, tres
cuatro, cinco, seis
and then I whisper
siete, ocho,
nueve,
diez.

## Estrellas

Tras la ventana
las estrellas de la noche esperan.
Cuento
uno, dos, tres,
cuatro, cinco, seis
y luego susurro
siete, ocho,
nueve,
diez.

—Lori Marie Carlson
*translated from the English
by L. M. C.*